✦Sam's Christmas Wish✦

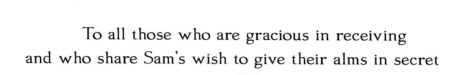

To all those who are gracious in receiving
and who share Sam's wish to give their alms in secret
—GD

To my sister Danette and her sweet family,
John, James, and Emily,
in remembrance of all our childhood Christmases
—DB

Library of Congress Cataloging-in-Publication Data
Durrant, George D., author.
   Sam's Christmas wish / George Durrant ; illustrated by Dan Burr.
      pages cm
   Summary: Sam has been grumpy ever since he lost his job and he shows it most when he warns everyone that if any "do-gooders" try to help his family during the Christmas holidays, he will be waiting for them with a shotgun in his lap.
   ISBN 978-1-60907-606-1 (hardbound : alk. paper)
[1. Christmas—Fiction. 2. Gifts—Fiction. 3. Conduct of life—Fiction. 4. Christian life—Fiction.] I. Burr, Dan, 1960–illustrator. II. Title.
   PZ7.D93426 Sam 2014
   [E]—dc23   2014012898

Printed in the United States of America   06/2014
Publishers Printing, Salt Lake City, UT

10 9 8 7 6 5 4 3 2 1

Sam's Christmas Wish

George D. Durrant

illustrated by **Dan Burr**

SHADOW
MOUNTAIN

Big Sam Edwards had been grumpy ever since he lost his job a few weeks before Christmas. He was worried about "do-gooders" meddling during the holidays. "We don't need no charity," he grumbled. He made a few phone calls and gruffly warned, "I'll be watching if anybody comes around trying to leave anything at the door!"

On Christmas Eve, after his wife, Kathryn, and his children had gone to bed, Sam sat in his small front room with a shotgun in his lap. After a couple of hours, his eyelids grew heavy, and soon Sam was asleep.

The next morning, Sam awoke to the shouts of his children: "Daddy, Daddy, look what Santa left us!" Sam rubbed his eyes. He could hardly believe what he saw. Gifts were piled all around him. On the table rested a large ham, and a Bible lay open under a miniature Christmas tree. For an instant the tiniest of smiles crept across Sam's face as he remembered his own childhood at Christmastime. But the thought vanished as quickly as it had come when Sam remembered his family's grim situation.

Sam stiffened. He jumped from his chair and shouted, "Don't touch those things! This is not our stuff, and somebody is going to pay for poking their nose into my business." He ran to the front door to check the lock. Pulling it open, he scowled at another pile of gifts on the doorstep.

Sam quickly went to the telephone and called his longtime friend, Sheriff Walt Durrant. "Sheriff," he blurted, "you get over here! Somebody broke into my house, and I want them arrested."

As he slammed the phone down, Sam noticed that his children were still gazing at the pile of toys. "You kids get back to bed," he ordered.

Hanging their heads, the children retreated. Kathryn closed her lips together tightly and went into the kitchen to start cooking some oatmeal. Breakfast might be the best meal they were going to have that day.

Thirty-five minutes later, Sheriff Durrant arrived. He got an earful as Sam explained what had happened.

"Did they take anything?" the sheriff asked.

"No, but I'm fed up with all the do-gooders in this town. I can take care of myself and my family. I don't need help from nobody."

The sheriff scratched his head and said, "Funny thing is, when I drove down your lane from the road, I could see that nobody else had been down here since the big snow last night."

"That's impossible," Sam huffed.

"Go see for yourself," the sheriff smiled.

After searching the front and back of the house, Sam shouted, "Somebody's raked over the tracks."

"Nonsense," said the sheriff. "Nobody has been here." Speaking as softly and as kindly as he could, Sheriff Durrant said, "Look, Sam, I've got Christmas waiting at home. Why don't you just take the stuff and enjoy it? Just be grateful."

Sam stared at him. He couldn't bring himself to say anything. He swallowed hard and waved good-bye as the sheriff drove away.

Sam slowly walked back into the house and sat in his chair.

Kathryn said softly, "Sam, what does it matter how it got here? It's here."

The children clustered in the doorway, hopeful looks on their faces. Six-year-old Katie hopped from one foot to another, her face alive with a sudden idea: "Daddy, maybe there's some tracks on top of the house!"

Then it him like a light! Some troublemaker had actually rented a helicopter and landed on his roof!

Sam ran to the shed, grabbed a wooden ladder, and propped it against the side of the house. He bolted to the top and looked carefully around, but he saw nothing.

Little Katie called to him, "Are there any reindeer tracks?"

Sam paused and looked down at her and her brother. A feeling came over him—the same feeling he had felt when he had first awakened and seen the gifts surrounding him in his chair. The spirit of Christmas overwhelmed him as he said with a chuckle, "Yeah, I think I can see some reindeer tracks over by the chimney. What are you kids waiting for? Those toys must be for you!"

Soon the ham was cooking in the oven. The children were playing with their toys. The miniature Christmas tree was on the table. Unnoticed by his family, Sam picked up the open Bible. A verse was underlined. He read: "That thine alms may be in secret: and thy Father which seeth in secret himself shall reward thee openly."

Never before or since has more joy been packed into one little house or into one father's heart than there was at that moment.

Over the next thirty-six years, almost everyone in town was touched by one of Sam's kindnesses. And Sheriff Durrant and Sam became the closest of friends.

In conversations with the sheriff, Sam would often nudge him and say, "You remember that Christmas when there was no tracks nowhere? I just wish I could do like Jesus said in the Bible. I wish I could do something good and do it in secret so nobody would ever know."

The sheriff would smile and say, "Maybe someday, Sam."

Sam grew old. Arthritis in his legs made it difficult for him to get up and around. He missed his wife, who had passed away years earlier. He missed his children, who had started families of their own. They would come for Christmas and other occasions, but it wasn't like having them there all the time.

One Christmas Eve, Sam was settling in for an evening alone when the Gentry family came caroling. Their frequent visits would always put a smile on Sam's face. He loved that they lived nearby, just across the field.

After their song, four-year-old Ben Gentry hugged Sam like he was a giant teddy bear and said, "We love you, Grandpa Sam. Merry Christmas."

Later that night, Sam sat by his window, watching thick snowflakes cover the countryside in a blanket of white. It was so peaceful. But suddenly, as he looked across the open field, he realized to his horror that the Gentrys' house was on fire.

Struggling from his chair, he stumbled out the back door, pushed through the gate in the fence, and hurried toward the burning house. The pains in his legs made it difficult for him to walk, but Sam didn't let that stop him. He had to help the Gentrys.

The flames had engulfed nearly the entire home. Near the front of the house Sam heard Mrs. Gentry scream, "Bennie is still in there!"

The boy's father shouted, "I'll try again!"

However, two neighbors grabbed him, yelling, "You can't go back! It's too dangerous."

Unnoticed by anyone, Sam stepped through the back door. Flames and heat surrounded him, and the smoke choked his lungs, but he fought his way into the room. Finally, he heard a faint cough. He groped toward the sound and found little Ben lying on the floor. He scooped him up in his arms and forced his way to the back door. Placing the little boy down on the snow, Sam told him to go to the front of the house, where his mother would be waiting for him. Through the falling snow, with the last of his strength, Sam limped back to his home.

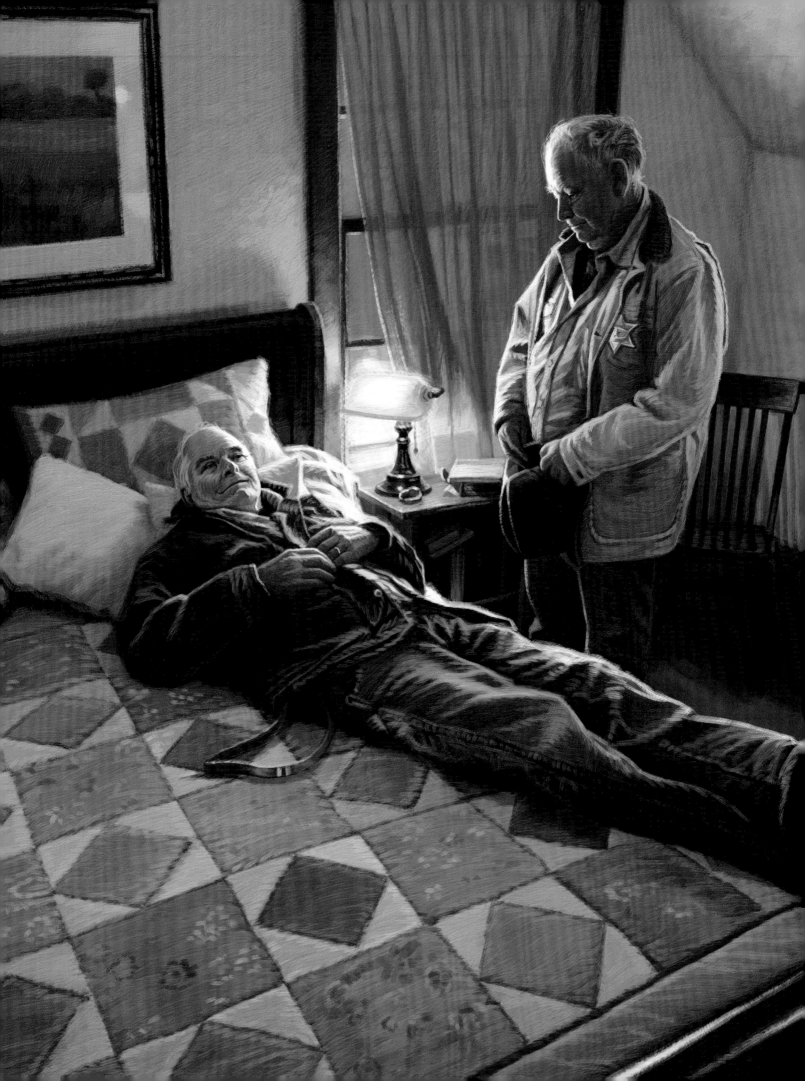

It was very late when Sheriff Durrant came into Sam's house. He found Sam lying fully dressed on his bed. "Sam, are you all right?" he said softly. "Did you go to the Gentrys' tonight? Their house caught on fire, and they thought that little Bennie was trapped inside, but then he appeared out of nowhere. The only thing Bennie whispered through all his coughing was your name, Sam. But there aren't any tracks outside your home, and I know your arthritis makes it difficult for you to walk. It couldn't have been you, right?"

An almost indistinguishable smile crossed Sam's face. Then his head fell to the side. Sam Edwards had died.

The next day, the sheriff was the last to leave Sam's house. Many people had come and gone, and now the house was empty. After locking the door, the sheriff turned toward the snow-covered field and paused. He missed his old friend already. A tear ran down his cheek. But a warm feeling filled his heart as he seemed to hear Sam's voice saying, "I finally did it, Sheriff. My wish came true. Merry Christmas."